Bullies Beware!
by Paul M. Kramer

This book is dedicated to all the millions of people
who were bullied at one time or another.

Bullies Beware! by Paul M. Kramer

© Paul M. Kramer August 2010. All Rights Reserved.

Aloha Publishers LLC
333 Dairy Road, Suite 106
Kahului, HI 96732
www.alohapublishers.com

Inquiries, comments or further information are available at, www. alohapublishers.com.

Illustrations by Mari Kuwayama greenwing001@hotmail.com.

ISBN 13 (EAN): 978-0-9819745-7-6   Printed in China
Library of Congress Control Number (LCCN): 2009934843

Bullies Beware!

by Paul M. Kramer

Aloha
PUBLISHERS
Books & Stories by Paul M. Kramer

It was Mikey's first day going to a new school.

Unexpectedly, two large boys jumped out in front of him.

One was named Jonathan, and the other named Jim.

They said, "If you give us some money, we will let you go through."

Mikey said, "Absolutely not to the both of you!"

"I am not stupid and I am not a fool, what you are doing is against the rules."

"You cannot take my money or stop me from going to school."

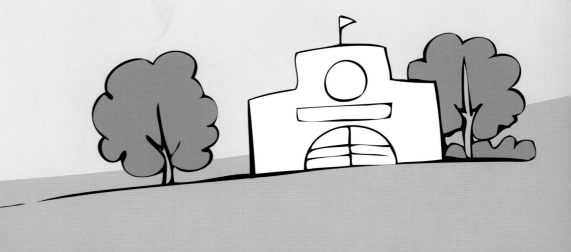

"We can and we will if that's what we want to."

"We have done it before and we'll do it again."

"Just ask Nicholas or Jeffrey or Peter or Ben."

"So give us some money or we'll give you a welcome
to our school punch."

"If you do not have any money, then give us your lunch."

"I will not give you anything," said Mikey, "So go away, skidoo!"

"Now leave me alone and let me pass through!"

Mikey received a shot to the arm and was pushed to the ground with a roar.

He tried to fight back but the bullies were too strong for him.

It was too hard to hold back both Jonathan and Jim.

Mikey yelled, "Stop, it's two against one!"

The bullies didn't care for they were having too much fun.

They gave Mikey a warning and said, "This warning do not ignore."

"Tomorrow bring us some money or we will hit you some more."

Mikey was scared; tears ran down from his eyes.

Easy it was not, but he tried to be brave.

He certainly did not want to be anyone's slave.

Said Jonathan to Jim, "That's enough for today, tomorrow he'll be back, he is not going away."

Mikey wiped his tears with his hand so his face would be dry.

Mikey did not want those bad boys to see him cry.

Mikey was restless and slept poorly that night.

He tossed and he turned and thought of what he should do.

What would you have done, if it happened to you?

Should he have told his teacher or his mother?

Should he have asked for help from his older brother?

He could not make up his mind, but something wasn't quite right.

Mikey knew that very next day he might have to fight.

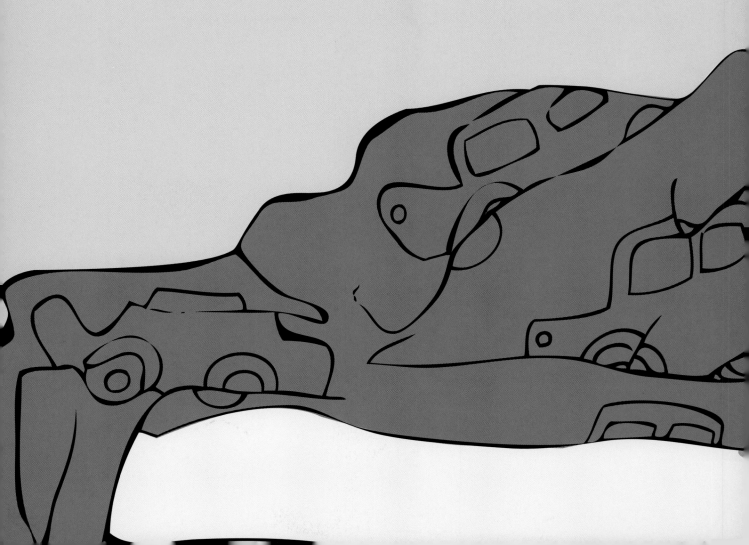

Mikey asked his mother to take him, do you know where?

She said, "She would if she could, but she could not."

Mikey began to worry and felt his face getting hot.

He knew he had to pass both Jonathan and Jim.

If he had nothing to give them, they were going to hurt him.

Mikey walked quickly and pretended he had not a care.

Mikey did not want to show them that he had any fear.

Jonathan grabbed Mikey's shirt as he tried to slip away.

Mikey let out a great big groan.

Then Mikey screamed; "Let me go, leave me alone!"

The bullies did not care as they pulled Mikey's hair.

Mikey shouted, "Why are you doing this, it just isn't fair!"

"If you let me go," said Mikey, "Tomorrow I will pay."

"Do we have a deal?" Jonathan and Jim both said, "Okay."

Mikey wished he was taller and not quite so slim.

Mikey lost his appetite and did not feel like eating.

He had wished that he had not made the deal and had taken the beating.

Unable to back out, there wasn't much he could do.

He would live up to his promise and try to see it through.

He thought if he were only bigger no one would pick on him, for he did not want to be afraid of either Jonathan or Jim.

The next day Mikey was ready to pay what was due.

Said Mikey to the bullies, "How long will this dollar last for?"

Jonathan said, "For a week and not for a day more."

"We are glad you decided to see it our way."

"We would now like to wish you a wonderful day."

Mikey replied, "I am sorry but I can't say the same to you."

"For I hope you have a terrible day, whatever you do."

Weeks later Mikey heard about a great new karate school.

Mikey asked his mother if he could please attend.

"My family, my friends and myself, I'll be able to defend."

"Let me go, let me go, please mother let me go!"

Mikey's mother said, "I know that you really want to go, so I will not tell you no."

Taking karate lessons for Mikey would be mighty cool.

Learning self defense and how to fight back would really rule.

Mikey started with a white belt, then a yellow and then a green.

To karate school Mikey went twice each and every week.

His instructor was a hard working man named Mr. Andrew Zeek.

He taught Mikey how to block, how to fall and how to kick.

Mikey learned how to use his strength as well as how to break a brick.

Constant exercising made Mikey like a finely tuned machine.

He was stronger, he was taller, but Mikey was not mean.

"I won't give you anymore money, "Mikey told the bullies this day.

Mikey had finally decided to end the deal with Jonathan and Jim.

No longer was Mikey going to let them bully him.

The bullies looked surprised and wondered what was up.

They asked, "If anyone put something strange in Mikey's milk cup."

"We strongly suggest that you do what we say."

Mikey said, "I will not, and starting today, I will no longer pay."

"I am not going to run, nor will I hide; I will face up to the both of you.

Jonathan said, "Your original lesson you have not learned yet,"

"This time you will not forget the beating you are about to get."

"But now it's getting late, so let us meet at ten after three."

"We will see you in the school playground by the very large tree,"

Mikey replied, "At the very large tree at ten after three is fine with me too."

A few kids told a few kids and later that day everybody knew.

Mikey pictured in his mind getting even with the bullies some day.

Jonathan and Jim couldn't push Mikey around as they used to.

Was fighting the bullies worth the trouble Mikey could get himself into?

Mikey decided to tell his teacher all the bad things they did to him.

That he was punched and pushed around by both Jonathan and Jim.

His teacher assured him that there would not be any fighting today.

She said, "To stop a bully from bullying; fighting was not the way."

A little after three by the very large tree a big crowd gathered round.

Many students and some friends of Mikey came to cheer for him.

At exactly ten after three came Jonathan and Jim.

Mikey was already waiting along with the principal and his teacher, Ms Caraway.

The principal told the crowd to go home, there was no need for anyone to stay,

The crowd quickly left the school playground.

Would those bullies now stop pushing Mikey around?

The principal told all three boys to be in his office 8AM the next day.

That night Mikey told his mother and brother what happened in school and about being bullied for almost a year.

He didn't tell them before because he was embarrassed and didn't want them to know that he was scared.

Mikey's mom said, "Don't ever be ashamed to tell me anything that's troubling you."

"I will try hard to understand everything you might be going through."

Mikey's mom was proud of him for his courage in confiding in Ms. Caraway.

He got a hug and a kiss from his mom who said everything will be okay.

The principal asked the bullies to tell him their version of the story.

Jonathan said, "We were joking and never meant to hurt him."

"We gladly accepted Mikey's weekly gift to us", uttered Jim.

The principal said, "Bullying was unacceptable and against the rules."

"Aggressive behavior will not be tolerated, especially not in school."

"Both of you need to take the responsibility for all that you do."

"If we did nothing, you wouldn't think we cared about you."

The very next day after Mikey arrived at school.

"Congratulations said this one, "You were very brave to tell,"
said that one, it seemed that the entire school knew.

Five different girls said to Mikey, I would like to go out with you.

It turned out that Jonathan and Jim did not attend school that day.

There was talk that both of their families were moving away.

It is sad that bullies do not get enough love or attention at home
which is certainly not very cool.

Most of the kids, especially the small and shy ones now looked up
to Mikey and said that Mikey rules.

Bullies

Displaying strength and power
Wanting you to be scared
Rule by force
Intimidation through fear

Hurting people's feelings
Taking advantage of the meek
Humiliating belittling threats
Victimizing the weak

Others feelings unimportant
Bulldozing anyone in the way
Frightening terrorizing traumatizing
Anyone not doing what they say

We know who you are

Paul M Kramer

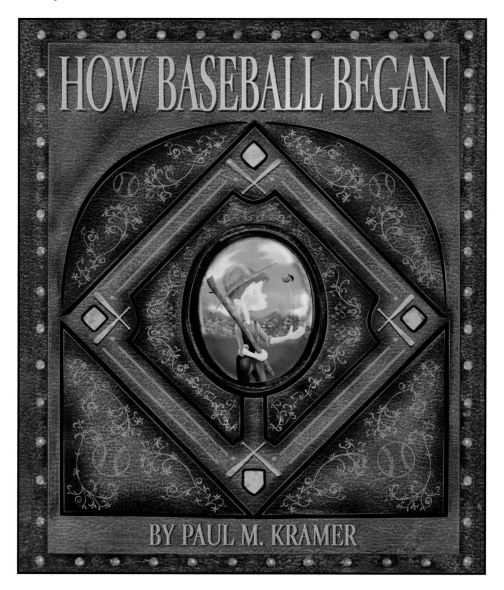

How Baseball Began – How did America's beloved game of baseball actually begin? This informative sweet story written in rhyme tells us. It educates newcomers about the fundamentals of the sport and the basic rules of the game. Both big and little leaguers will be entertained and delighted by the logical, step by step progress the story presents, from baseballs simple beginnings to the game we know today. The big question is, did baseball really begin the way Clem, Carl, and Fred said it did?

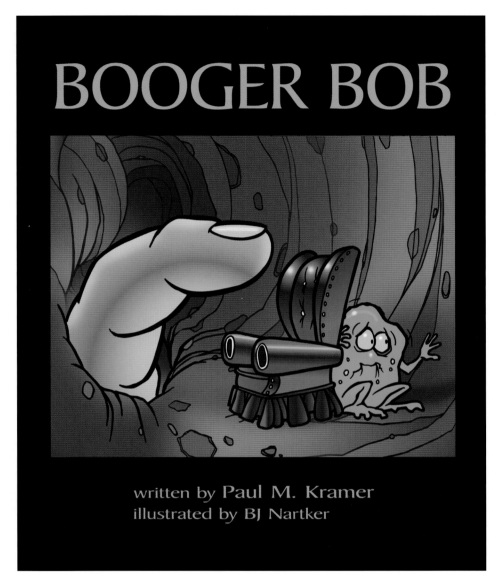

BOOGER BOB

written by Paul M. Kramer
illustrated by BJ Nartker

Booger Bob – It is difficult to teach children proper personal hygiene. This cute story is a funny representation of what people do with what comes out of their noses and how they dispose of it. Although the subject matter could be considered gross by many, there is a lesson to be learned after the laughter stops.

About the Author

Paul M Kramer lives in Hawaii on the Island of Maui, but was born and raised in New York City. He moved to the Rainbow and Aloha State of Hawaii in 1995 with his wife Cindy and their then infant son, Lukas. After being in Hawaii for about nine years, Mr. Kramer's true passion in life was awakened. He began writing children's books that deal with important issues that kids face today. Mr. Kramer's books are written in rhyme, are easy to read and make learning fun.